KING OF THE SKY

NICOLA DAVIES

ILLUSTRATED BY LAURA CARLIN

FIRST U.S. EDITION 2017

LIBRARY OF CONGRESS CATALOG CARD NUMBER PENDING
ISBN 978-0-7636-9568-2

17 18 19 20 21 22 APS 10 9 8 7 6 5 4 3 2 1

PRINTED IN HUMEN, DONGGUAN, CHINA

THE TEXT IN THIS BOOK WAS HAND-LETTERED.
THE ILLUSTRATIONS WERE DONE IN MIXED MEDIA.

CANDLEWICK PRESS
99 DOVER STREET
SOMERVILLE, MASSACHUSETTS 02144

VISIT US AT WWW.CANDLEWICK.COM

CANDLEWICK PRESS

For all children who have to find home in a new place N.D.

FOR LIZZIE   L.C.

IT RAINED AND RAINED AND RAINED.
LITTLE HOUSES HUDDLED ON THE HUMPBACKED HILLS.
CHIMNEYS SMOKED AND METAL TOWERS CLANKED.
THE STREETS SMELLED OF MUTTON SOUP AND COAL DUST
AND NO ONE SPOKE MY LANGUAGE.

ALL OF IT TOLD ME **THIS** IS NOT WHERE YOU BELONG.

JUST ONE THING REMINDED ME OF HOME—
OF SUNLIGHT, FOUNTAINS, AND THE VANILLA SMELL
OF ICE CREAM IN MY NONNA'S GELATERIA.
IT WAS MR. EVANS'S PIGEONS IN THEIR LOFT BEHIND MY HOUSE,
COOING AS IF THEY STRUTTED IN ST. PETER'S SQUARE IN ROME.

MR. EVANS'S FACE WAS CRUMPLED AND HE COULD HARDLY WALK,
BUT WHEN HIS BIRDS FLEW, HE SMILED LIKE SPRINGTIME.

I STOOD BESIDE HIM AND WATCHED
AS HIS PIGEONS SOARED ABOVE THE CHIMNEYS AND THE TOWERS,
UP TO WHERE THE SKY STRETCHED ALL THE WAY TO ITALY.

A LIFETIME WORKING IN A COAL MINE
HAD TAKEN MR. EVANS'S BREATH AWAY,
SO HE SPOKE SOFT AND SLOW,
SLOW ENOUGH FOR ME TO UNDERSTAND.

"I LIKE TO SEE THEM FLY," HE WHISPERED,
"AFTER SO LONG UNDERGROUND."

EVERY DAY I CAME TO SEE THE PIGEONS.
"I'M TRAINING THEM TO RACE," MR. EVANS SAID,
"AND THIS ONE'S **GOING TO BE A CHAMPION."**
HE PUT A PIGEON IN MY HANDS.

I FELT ITS SMALL HEART RACING UNDERNEATH MY FINGER
AND THE PUSH AND POWER OF ITS WINGS.
ITS HEAD WAS WHITER THAN A SPLASH OF MILK. ITS EYE BLAZED FIRE.
"NAME HIM AND HE'S YOURS," THE OLD MAN SAID.

I DIDN'T HAVE TO THINK. "RE DEL CIELO!" I REPLIED.

"KING OF THE SKY!"

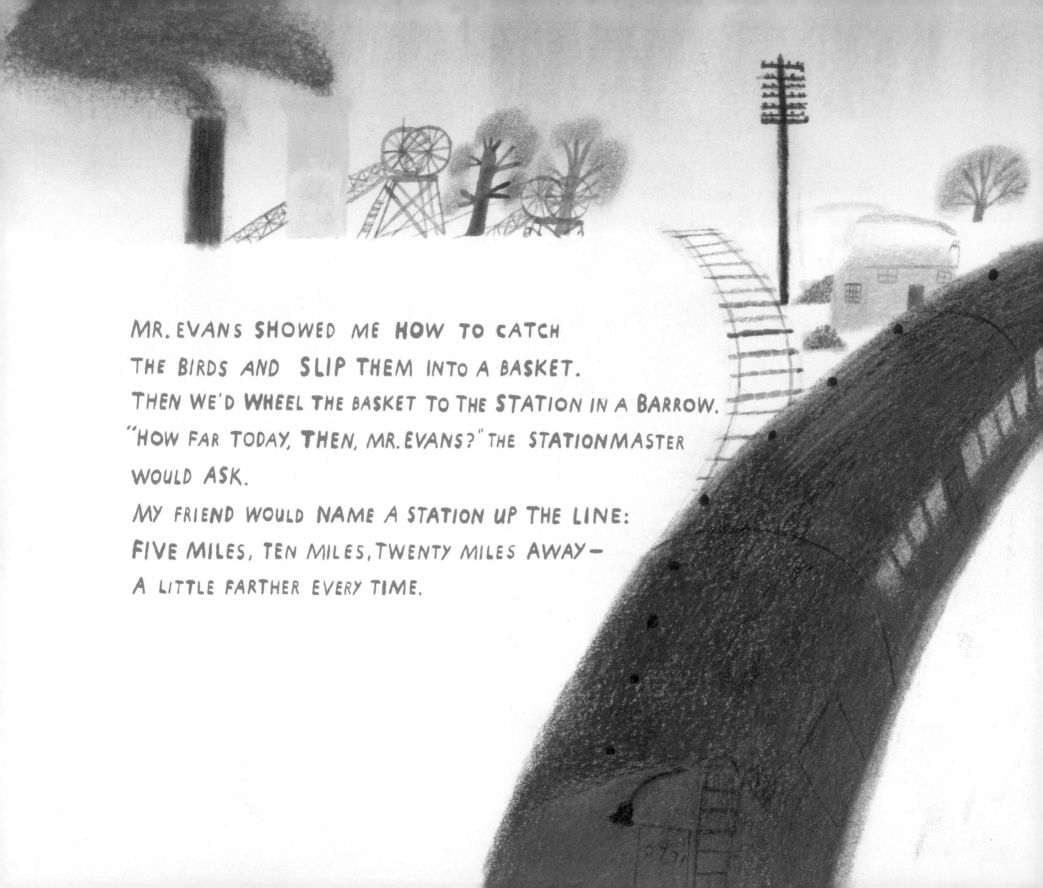

MR. EVANS SHOWED ME HOW TO CATCH
THE BIRDS AND SLIP THEM INTO A BASKET.
THEN WE'D WHEEL THE BASKET TO THE STATION IN A BARROW.
"HOW FAR TODAY, THEN, MR. EVANS?" THE STATIONMASTER
WOULD ASK.
MY FRIEND WOULD NAME A STATION UP THE LINE:
FIVE MILES, TEN MILES, TWENTY MILES AWAY—
A LITTLE FARTHER EVERY TIME.

"THEY DON'T NEED A MAP LIKE WE DO," MR. EVANS TOLD ME.
"THEY'RE BORN KNOWING HOW TO FIND THEIR WAY.
ALL THEY NEED IS A BIT OF PRACTICE."

BACK AT THE LOFT, WE'D WAIT, EATING MRS. EVANS'S WELSH CAKES
AND SQUINTING UP INTO THE LIGHT.
"LOOK OUT NOW!" MR. EVANS WOULD SAY. "KEEP THOSE YOUNG EYES OF YOURS WELL PEELED!"
IT NEVER TOOK THEM LONG.
FROM PLACES FAR AWAY, PLACES THAT THEY'D NEVER BEEN,
THE PIGEONS FLEW HOME STRAIGHT AND FAST AS ARROWS.

BUT THE PIGEON WITH THE MILK-WHITE HEAD WAS ALWAYS LAST.

STILL MR. EVANS SAID HE'D BE A WINNER.

"HE'S A HERO," THE OLD MAN WHEEZED, "LIKE THE PIGEONS IN THE WAR, CARRYING MESSAGES EVEN WHEN THEY WERE SHOT. JUST YOU WAIT AND SEE!"

EVERY DAY MR. EVANS GREW A LITTLE WEAKER.
BY RACING SEASON HE COULDN'T LEAVE HIS BED.
SO I PUT THE RACE RINGS ON THE PIGEONS' LEGS
AND TOOK THEM TO THE STATION.
I SCOURED THE SKY FOR THEIR RETURN AND CHECKED THEM IN.

MR. EVANS'S BEDROOM **WALL** WAS PAPERED WITH THEIR WINNINGS—
BUT NOT ONE FOR RE DEL **CIELO**, MY KING OF THE SKY.
"HE'S GOT THE WINGS FOR DISTANCE," MR. EVANS BREATHED.
"HERE'S THE RACE HE'S WAITED FOR."

HE HANDED **ME THE** ENTRY FOR**M**:
KING OF THE SKY WOULD GO TO **ROME** BY TRAIN,
THEN RACE BACK A THOUSAND MILES AND MORE!

I SMOOTHED HIS FEATHERS, LOOKED INTO HIS EYE,
AND PUT HIM INTO THE BASKET FOR THE JOURNEY.
A PART OF ME WAS GOING WITH HIM.
I WASN'T SURE IT WOULD COME BACK.

THE RACE DAY DAWNED. A STORM BLEW IN.

LIGHTNING, WIND, AND RAIN.

I WAITED FOR **TWO WHOLE DAYS** AND **NIGHTS,** BUT THE **PIGEON**
WITH **THE MILK-WHITE HEAD DID NOT RETURN.**

I SAT BESIDE MY FRIEND'S BED,
AND I TOLD HIM

THAT PERHAPS THE SUNLIGHT AND THE FOUNTAINS
AND THE VANILLA SMELL OF ICE CREAM
FROM A THOUSAND GELATERIE
HAD MADE OUR PIGEON WANT TO STAY.

"NO!" SAID MR. EVANS.
"THAT WILL ONLY TELL HIM...
THIS IS NOT WHERE YOU BELONG."

THE OLD MAN'S EYES **BLAZED** FIRE.
"GET OUT THERE, BOY," HE SAID,
"AND WELCOME **HIM!**"

THE RAIN HAD STOPPED. I RAN **OUT** TO THE LOFT
AND SQUINTED UP INTO THE CLOUDS.
A SPECK... A BLOB... A BIRD.
A PIGEON WITH A MILK-WHITE HEAD,
A HERO AND A CHAMPION!

TWELVE HUNDRED MILES HE'D FLOWN,
FROM SOMEWHERE FAR AWAY HE'D NEVER BEEN.
STEERED NORTH AND WEST, FINDING HIS DIRECTION FROM THE SUN
AND THE FORCE THAT GUIDES A COMPASS NEEDLE.
FLOWN UNTIL HE SAW THE SHAPE OF HUMPBACKED HILLS,
THE LINES OF LITTLE HOUSES AND THE CHIMNEYS,
HEARD THE CLANKING TOWERS, SMELLED THE SOUP AND COAL DUST.

FLOWN DOWN INTO THE ARMS
OF THE SMILING, CRYING BOY—
THE BOY WHO KNEW AT LAST
THAT HE WAS HOME.